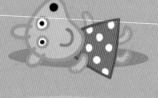

First published by Ladybird Books Ltd 2009
This edition published by Ladybird Books Ltd 2010
A Penguin Company
Penguin Books Ltd, 80 Strand, London, WC2R 0RL, UK
Penguin Books Australia Ltd, Camberwell, Victoria, Australia
Penguin Group (NZ), 67 Apollo Drive, Rosedale, North Shore
0632, New Zealand (a division of Pearson New Zealand Ltd)

www.ladybird.com

2 4 6 8 10 9 7 5 3 1
Printed in China

This book is based on the
TV Series 'Peppa Pig'
'Peppa Pig' is created by
Neville Astley and Mark Baker

Peppa Pig © Astley Baker Davies
Ltd/ E1 Entertainment 2003

www.peppapig.com

Dentist Trip

Every morning, Peppa and George brush their teeth. Scrub! Scrub! Scrub!

"George, are your teeth as clean as mine?" Peppa asks, showing off her clean white teeth.

"You both have lovely clean teeth. I'm sure the dentist will be happy!" calls out Daddy Pig.

Later that day, Peppa and George are at the dentists, waiting for their check-up. It is George's first visit.

"Peppa! George! The dentist will see you now!" says Miss Rabbit, the nurse. "Hooray!" they both cheer.

This is Doctor
Elephant, the dentist.
"Who's first?" he asks.

"I'm first," replies Peppa.
"I'm a big girl.
Watch me, George!"

13

"Open wide, please!" orders
Doctor Elephant, softly.
"Aaaaah . . ." Peppa opens her mouth
as wide as she possibly can.
"Let's take a look!" says the dentist,
checking Peppa's teeth with a mirror.

"There. All done! What lovely clean teeth!" cheers Doctor Elephant. "Now, you can have the special drink." Gargle! Ptooou! Peppa spits the pink liquid out into the sink. It's George's turn next.

George does not want it to be his turn. So the dentist lets him hold Mr Dinosaur. "All done. You have very strong, clean teeth, George!" smiles Doctor Elephant.

"But wait, what is this?" cries Doctor Elephant. "George has clean teeth, but this young dinosaur's teeth are very dirty."

"The water jet, please, Miss Rabbit!" orders the dentist. He uses the water to clean Mr Dinosaur's teeth. Slosh! Slosh! Slosh!

"Pink!" cries George, picking up a glass. "That's right, George!" says the dentist. "Mr Dinosaur needs some special pink drink!" Gurgle! Gurgle!

"Gosh! What shiny teeth you have, Mr Dinosaur!" cries Miss Rabbit. "Dine-saw! Grrr!" snorts George.

George loves Mr Dinosaur. Especially now that he has nice clean teeth.

Nature Trail

Peppa and her family are going on a
nature trail. Mummy Pig asks
Daddy Pig not to forget the picnic.
"As if I would," laughs Daddy Pig.

They head off along the
trail with their map.
Oh dear! Daddy Pig has left
the picnic in the car.

Mummy and Daddy Pig ask Peppa if she can
see anything interesting in the forest.
"I don't see anything but boring trees," says Peppa.
Then, she looks really hard and
finds some footprints on the ground.

"Let's follow the footprints and see who made them," says Mummy Pig. "We will have to be very quiet so we don't scare anything away. Shhhh!"

Peppa and George follow the footprints along the ground.
"It looks like they were made by a little bird," says Mummy Pig.

Soon, they come to the
end of the footprints.
"The bird has flown up into
that tree," smiles Daddy Pig.

"Where?" asks Peppa. Daddy Pig gives Peppa binoculars to help her see the bird.

The binoculars make everything look bigger. Peppa can see one, two, three baby birds!

"They're eating worms," says Peppa. "That's disgusting!"

George finds some more footprints. They are very little. Daddy Pig says they belong to ants collecting leaves to eat.

"I think it's time for lunch," says Mummy Pig. But Daddy Pig has left the picnic in the car!

"My map is wrong," begins Daddy Pig. "We'll have to follow our own footprints back to the car."

Suddenly, it starts to rain.
Everyone's footprints are washed away!
"How are we going to find the car, now?"
asks Mummy Pig.

Quack!   Quack!

"Ducks love picnics," says Peppa. "Mrs Duck, can you help us find our picnic please?"

The ducks lead Peppa and her family back to their car. "We're here! Thank you for your help Mrs Duck," cries Peppa.

"I love picnics!" laughs Daddy Pig. The ducks love picnics too. Quack! Quack! So do the birds!

And so do the ants!
Munch! Munch!
"Everybody loves picnics!"
cries Peppa.

Daddy Pig's Old Chair

The school roof has a hole in it. "We are going to have a jumble sale," announces Madame Gazelle.

"The money we raise will pay for a new roof."
Everybody has to bring something to sell.

Later, Peppa is in her bedroom choosing a toy to give
to the jumble sale. "Mr Dinosaur!" she decides.

Everybody gasps and George bursts into tears.
"You can't give away Mr Dinosaur," says Mummy Pig.

"Why don't you give your old jack-in-the-box?" suggests Daddy Pig.

"Oh. OK," agrees Peppa.
"Now it's your turn Daddy.
What are you going to give?"

Daddy Pig is not sure.

"What about your old squeaky chair?"

suggests Peppa helpfully.

"But it's very old and valuable," says Daddy Pig.
"Hee hee," says Mummy Pig. "You found it
on a rubbish tip!"

When Madame Gazelle arrives in her truck,
Mummy Pig, Peppa and George give her everything
to take to the jumble sale.

Naughty Mummy Pig gives her Daddy's
squeaky chair too.
"Daddy Pig will never notice,"
she whispers to Peppa.

It is the day of the jumble sale.
There are lots of things to buy.

Mummy Pig wants to buy some fruit and vegetables.
Daddy Pig wants to buy a chocolate cake.

"Peppa," says Miss Rabbit.
"How about buying this chair?
It's a bit of rubbish but you can chop
it up and use it for firewood."

"But Daddy says it's very old and worth lots of money!" says Peppa.

All Peppa's friends have given something to the jumble sale. Suzy has given her nurse's outfit.

Pedro has given his balloon and
Candy has given her aeroplane.

"I will miss my jack-in-the-box," sighs Peppa.
"I will miss playing at nurses," says Suzy sadly.

Peppa's friends all think they will miss their toys, so they buy them back again.

"Look what I've bought!" snorts Daddy Pig.
"It's an antique chair to match my old one!"

"Oh Daddy Pig!" laughs Mummy Pig.
"It matches your old one because it
IS your old one!" snorts Peppa.

"But Miss Rabbit has just charged me lots of money for it!" says poor Daddy Pig. "Fantastic news!" says Madame Gazelle.

"We have just raised all the money
we need for a new school roof!"
"Hooray!" everybody cheers.

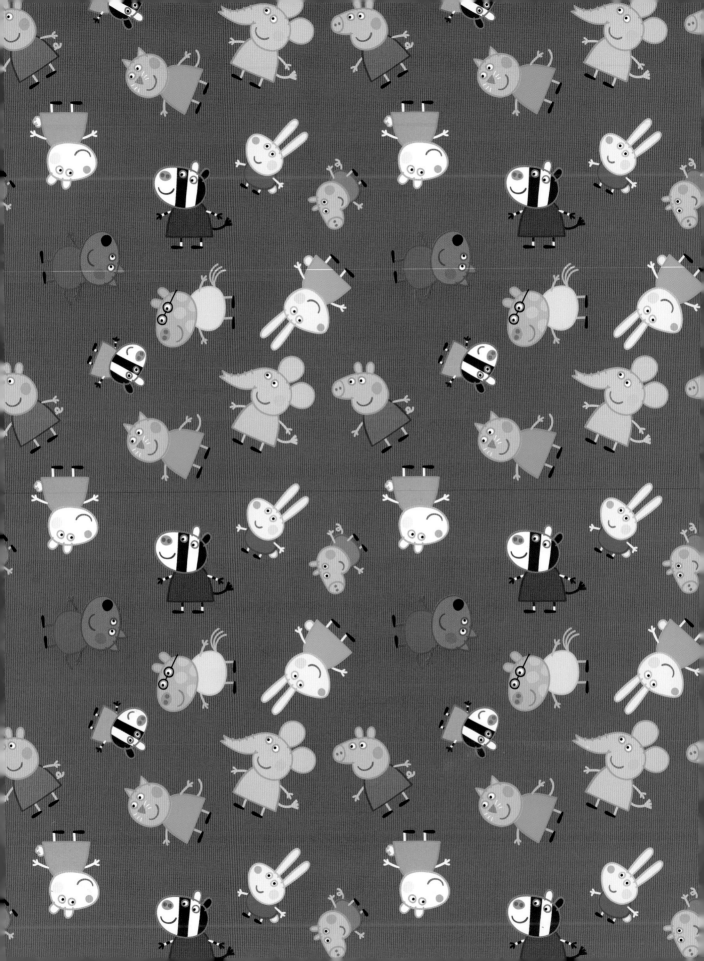

Recycling Fun

Mr Bull, the binman, is collecting the rubbish. It's early in the morning so he tries to be as quiet as he can.

Crash Clank!

But Mr Bull is not very good at being quiet.
"Hello Mr Bull," snort Daddy Pig, Peppa and George.

"Hello everyone," says Mr Bull.

81

Peppa and George are helping
to clear up the breakfast things.
"We don't put bottles in the rubbish bin.
They can be recycled," says Mummy Pig.

83

Soon they have collected enough things, so Peppa and her family set off for the recycle centre.

Mummy Pig has the bottles and Peppa has the tin cans. George has the newspapers.

"Is everybody ready?" asks Daddy Pig.
"Yes!" shout Peppa and George.

Clink, clink, rattle, rattle, rustle, rustle!

Soon, they arrive at Miss Rabbit's recycle centre.

Miss Rabbit is sitting high up inside a big crane.

She is busy recycling all the rusty old cars.

It is very noisy.

"Who knows which bin the bottles go in?" asks Mummy Pig.

"The green one!" says Peppa.
"That's right!" snorts Daddy Pig.
Clink! Clink!

"And the cans go in the blue one!" says Peppa.

"Well done, Peppa," smiles Mummy Pig.

Rattle! Rattle!

Daddy Pig lifts George up so he can empty the newspapers into the red bin.
Rustle! Rustle!

"Where's our car gone?" asks Daddy Pig. "Stand back!" shouts Miss Rabbit from up above them. Miss Rabbit is about to recycle Peppa's car!

"Stop!"
shouts Peppa.
"Our car isn't old
and rusty!"

"Ha! Ha! Silly me!" says Miss Rabbit.
"I just love recycling."
"So do we!" laughs Peppa.
"But we also love our little car!"

School Bus Trip

Peppa and her friends are going on a school bus trip. "Let's check you are all here," says Madame Gazelle. "Here!" cries Peppa.

Woof!

103

"Today," begins Madame Gazelle, "we are going on a trip to the mountains!"

Peppa and Suzy are
already a little hungry.
"Please can we eat our lunch now?"
they ask Madame Gazelle.

"Why not eat your apples and save the rest for the picnic?" she replies. Crunch! Crunch!

The bus has arrived at the foot of the mountain. The road is very steep! "Come on bus! You can make it!" everyone cheers.

Peppa and her friends have finally made it to the top of the mountain.

"Look at the view!" gasps Madame Gazelle. All the children look out over the valley.

"Wow!" sighs Peppa, loudly.
"Wow! Wow! Wow!" Peppa hears
in the distance.
"What was that?" she asks quietly.
"It's your echo, Peppa!"
replies Madame Gazelle.

"An echo is the sound you hear when you speak loudly in the mountains," explains Madame Gazelle. Grunt! Woof! Baaa! Snort!

115

Now it's time for a picnic lunch. Peppa loves picnics. Everyone loves picnics! Munch! Slurp! Munch! Yum! Yum!

"Where are the ducks?" asks Peppa, taking a bite of her sandwich. "They always turn up when we have picnics."

Quack! Quack! Quack!
Here come the ducks.
"Hello! Would you like some bread?"
Peppa asks them. The ducks are very
lucky today. There is plenty of bread!

The bus has arrived.
It's time to go home.
"Let's all sing a song!" suggests
Madame Gazelle. Hooray!
Everyone has had a great day!

Sports Day

Today is school sports day.

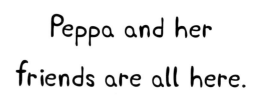

Peppa and her
friends are all here.

The first event is running.

The children have to run as fast as they can.

"Ready . . . Steady . . . Go!"
says Madame Gazelle.

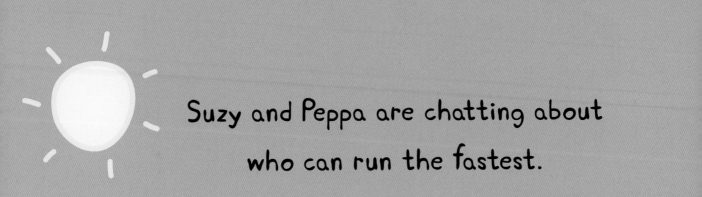

Suzy and Peppa are chatting about
who can run the fastest.

Rebecca Rabbit is in the lead.
Peppa and Suzy are right at the back.

Rebecca Rabbit wins the race!

"Hooray," everyone cheers.

Peppa and Suzy are last.

"It's not the winning that matters,"
Daddy Pig reminds them.
"But the taking part."

"The next event is the long jump," says Madame Gazelle.

George and Richard Rabbit have to run
and then jump as far as they can.
Whoever jumps the furthest is the winner.
"Ready . . . Steady . . . Go!"

Oh dear. Richard Rabbit has
jumped further than George.
"Hooray!" shout all his friends.

George is not happy.

"Remember George," says Peppa. "It's not the winning that matters but the taking part."

The next race is the relay.
Daddy Pig is in the lead. He hands
the baton to Peppa.

"Thank you Daddy, you did very well. Now it's my turn to. . . " begins Peppa. "Stop talking and run!" snorts Daddy Pig.

Emily Elephant is the winner!
Everyone cheers. "Hooray!"

Peppa comes last.
She is not feeling happy.

It's the last event of the day, the tug of war.

Boys against girls.

"The girls will win!" snorts Peppa.

"Woof! No they won't!" says Danny.
Everyone is pulling so hard, the rope breaks!

"The result is a draw!
Both teams win!" says Madame Gazelle.
Everybody cheers.

"Hooray!"

"I love school sports day," snorts Peppa,
"Especially when I win a prize!"

Peppa Goes Swimming

It's a lovely sunny day and Peppa and her family are at the swimming pool. "Peppa! George! Let Daddy put on your armbands," snorts Mummy Pig.

Today is George's first time at the pool and he's a bit scared of getting in.

"Why don't you just put one foot in the water?" suggests Daddy Pig.
"Maybe George should try both feet at the same time?" says Mummy Pig.

Splash! Mummy Pig convinces George to jump into the water and he loves it! "Grunt! Hee! Hee! Snort!" shouts George, happily. "Ho! Ho! Well done, George!" snorts Daddy Pig.

Here is Rebecca Rabbit with her brother, Richard and their mummy.

"Hello, everyone!" cries Rebecca.
"Squeak, squeak," says Richard.

"Richard, hold on to this float and you can practise kicking your legs," says Mummy Rabbit. "George, would you like to try kicking your legs?" asks Mummy Pig. "Hee! Hee! Float! Snort!" giggles George.

"Ho! Ho! Very good," laughs Daddy Pig,
"but please try not to splash."
"Grunt! Big children don't splash," adds Peppa.

"Big children are very good at swimming," snorts Peppa. "When George and Richard are older, they'll be able to swim like us, won't they, Rebecca?"

"Yes!" says Rebecca, as she watches the boys kicking.

Peppa and Rebecca race each other up and down the pool with their armbands on.

They are having lots of fun swimming and splashing in the water.

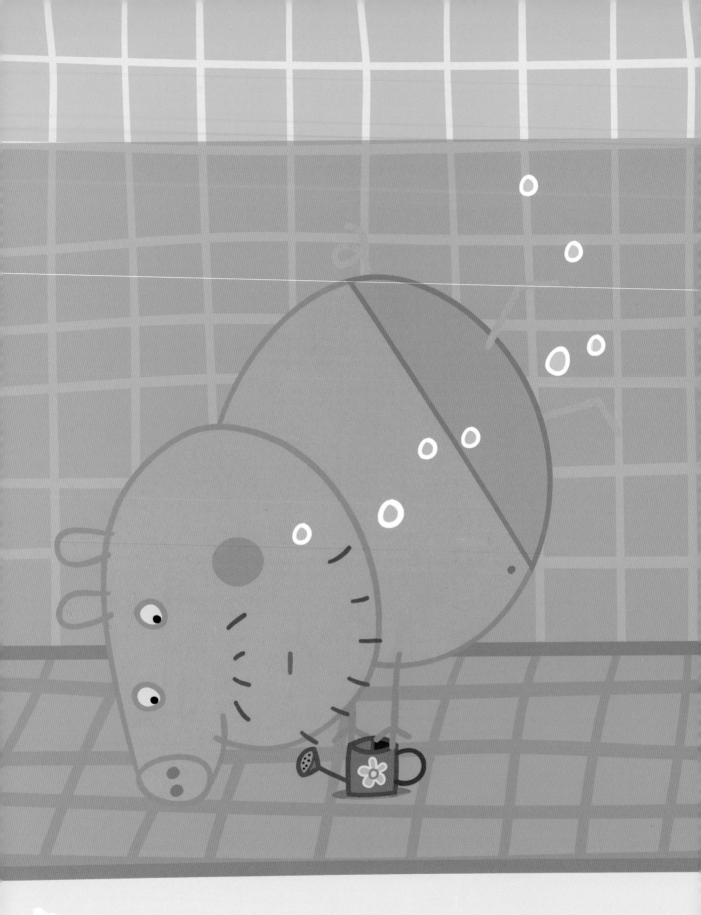

Oops! Richard has dropped his toy
watering can into the pool.
"Mummy! Wah!" cries Richard.
"Sorry, Richard, I can't reach.
It's too far down," says Mummy Rabbit.
Luckily, Daddy Pig is an excellent swimmer.
He takes off his glasses and dives down to get it.

"Ho! Ho! There you go!"
snorts Daddy Pig.
"Squeak, squeak!" says Richard.

"Well done, Daddy!" smiles Mummy Pig.

169

Oh dear! Now Richard is soaking Daddy Pig with the watering can. What a naughty Rabbit! "He! He! He!" George thinks it's hilarious. Everyone has had a wonderful day at the pool!

Tiny Creatures

Peppa and George are helping Grandpa Pig pick vegetables. Grandpa hands Peppa a lettuce.

Peppa can see something sitting on the lettuce. "There's a horrible monster!" she snorts.

"That's just a little snail!"
says Grandpa.
"Grrr. Mon-sta!" says George.

George likes the snail.

Suddenly the snail disappears.

"Where's he gone?" asks Peppa.

"He's hiding in his shell," explains Grandpa.

"Grandpa! George and
I want to be snails,"
says Peppa.

"Well," says Grandpa, "these baskets can be your shells!"
"I'm going to eat up all Grandpa Pig's lettuce!" laughs Peppa.

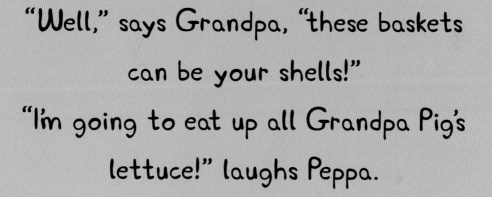

"Oi! Keep off my lovely lettuce you cheeky snails!" calls Grandpa.

"And when Grandpa Pig shouts at me," giggles Peppa,

"I'll hide inside my little house!"

"Mon-sta!" says George.

Here are Peppa and George's friends. "Can we be snails too?" they ask.

"Well," says Grandpa. "You could be something else exciting from the garden." "What's that buzzing sound?" asks Peppa.

"It's coming from that little house," says Suzy.

"It's a bee house," explains Grandpa.

"It's called a hive."

"The bees collect nectar from the flowers and then fly to the hive to make it into honey."

"Hmmmm, I like honey," says Peppa.
"Let's pretend to be bees!
Buzz buzz buzz ha ha ha!"
"What busy bees!" laughs Grandpa.

Granny Pig has been baking bread.

"Would you busy bees like some toast?" she asks.

"Yes please!" say Peppa and her friends.
"With lots of honey!"

"I like being a bee because they eat lots of lovely honey!" says Suzy.

"I like being a snail," snorts Peppa,
"because they eat all
Grandpa's vegetables!"

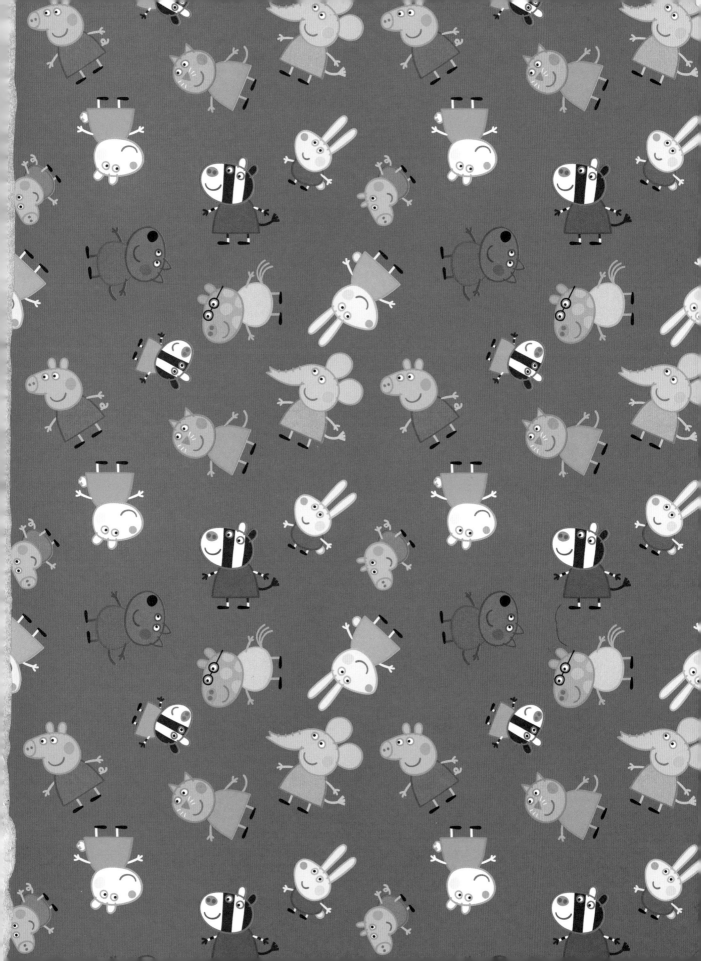

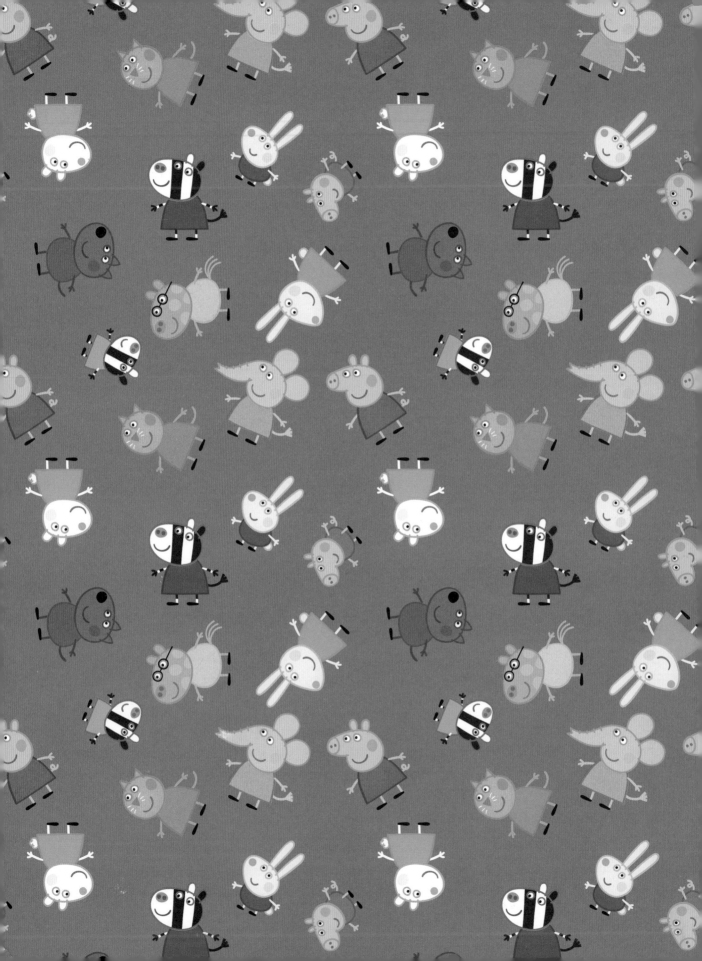